FAMILY FEUD

Bobbie chewed the inside of her lip. "If you're coming with me, you better get ready. I'm leaving in a half hour. I already fed your horse. He's the strawberry roan in the pen. Saddles are in the tack shed."

Bobbie moved past her cousin and grabbed a tarp off a peg on the wall. She took it outside and wrapped it in her bedroll.

In a few minutes Alex returned, leading the roan. Bobbie frowned. The horse's back was still bare. "I told you the saddles are in the tack shed—over there."

"All I could find were Western saddles. I'm used to riding English."

"You mean those itty-bitty things with hardly any leather on 'em and no saddle horn?"

Alex nodded.

"Look, Al, we're not going on an Easter egg hunt. We're looking for stray cattle. Some of them are mean and all of them are wild. You'll be spending all day in the saddle. Maybe you should tell Grandpa you want to stay here until I get back. It'll only be a week."

"You wish." Alex turned and led the roan toward the tack shed again. "Don't worry about me, hotshot. If you can handle it, so can I."

OTHER YEARLING BOOKS YOU WILL ENJOY:

JOURNEY, *Patricia MacLachlan*
SHILOH, *Phyllis Reynolds Naylor*
MISSING MAY, *Cynthia Rylant*
THE SECRET FUNERAL OF SLIM JIM THE SNAKE,
  Elvira Woodruff
AWFULLY SHORT FOR THE FOURTH GRADE,
  Elvira Woodruff
THE SUMMER I SHRANK MY GRANDMOTHER,
  Elvira Woodruff
HOW TO EAT FRIED WORMS, *Thomas Rockwell*
HOW TO FIGHT A GIRL, *Thomas Rockwell*
HOW TO GET FABULOUSLY RICH, *Thomas Rockwell*
BEETLES, LIGHTLY TOASTED, *Phyllis Reynolds Naylor*

YEARLING BOOKS are designed especially to entertain
and enlighten young people. Patricia Reilly Giff,
consultant to this series, received her bachelor's
degree from Marymount College and a master's
degree in history from St. John's University. She
holds a Professional Diploma in Reading and a
Doctorate of Humane Letters from Hofstra
University. She was a teacher and reading
~~~~~~ years, and is the author of

rling titles,

P.O. Box 1045,
South Holland, IL 60473.

GARY PAULSEN
WORLD OF ADVENTURE

HOOK 'EM, SNOTTY!

A YEARLING BOOK

Published by
Bantam Doubleday Dell Books for Young Readers
a division of
Bantam Doubleday Dell Publishing Group, Inc.
1540 Broadway
New York, New York 10036

ISBN: 0-440-41027-4

Series design: Barbara Berger

Interior illustration by Michael David Biegel

Printed in the United States of America

June 1995

10   9   8   7   6   5   4   3   2   1

OPM

Dear Readers:

Real adventure is many things—it's danger and daring and sometimes even a struggle for life or death. From competing in the Iditarod dogsled race across Alaska to sailing the Pacific Ocean, I've experienced some of this adventure myself. I try to capture this spirit in my stories, and each time I sit down to write, that challenge is a bit of an adventure in itself.

You're all a part of this adventure as well. Over the years I've had the privilege of talking with many of you in schools, and this book is the result of hearing firsthand what you want to read about most—power-packed action and excitement.

You asked for it—so hang on tight while we jump into another thrilling story in my World of Adventure.

Gary Paulsen

HOOK 'EM, SNOTTY!

CHAPTER 1

Bobbie Walker slapped her worn-out cowboy hat against the leg of her faded jeans. It caused a small cloud of dust but she didn't notice. Something else had her attention. Her grandpa's old white Ford pickup was rumbling up the road toward the Rocking W Ranch.

The day she had dreaded was finally here. Bobbie's cousin from Los Angeles was coming to the ranch to visit for a few weeks. Grandpa had left early this morning to go to the airport in Winston—nearly seventy-five miles away.

Bobbie had refused to go along. She wanted

it well understood from the start that bringing Alex out here wasn't her idea. The last thing they needed right now was a city greenhorn getting in the way of the annual wild cow roundup.

The old truck stopped in front of the house. Bobbie pulled her hat down low and moved away from the corrals. She walked to the bed of the pickup and lifted out her cousin's expensive leather suitcase.

The passenger door opened. A tall, slender girl with long brown hair, the same color as Bobbie's, stepped out. Her hair was parted on the side and she moved it off her face with her hand.

Bobbie looked her up and down. She wasn't impressed and it showed. The girl was wearing tight black shorts and a black T-shirt that said PRODUCT OF THE CITY. Bobbie winced when she noticed her cousin's feet.

Sandals.

One side of Bobbie's mouth went up. It always twitched like that when she didn't like something. She barely nodded at the girl and started for the house.

"Bobbie."

It was Grandpa. His voice held a note of displeasure. "Yes, sir?"

The tips of his thumb and forefinger smoothed down his gray handlebar mustache. "I want you to say hello to your cousin Alex."

Bobbie turned. Alex gave her a bored look under nearly closed eyelids. Bobbie shifted the suitcase and halfheartedly stuck out her hand.

Alex folded her arms in front of her. "I wouldn't want you to strain yourself."

Bobbie put her hand down.

"Gramps tells me there's a lot to do out here in the sticks." Alex cocked her head. "What do you do for fun, cousin, wait till Saturday night and count the flies on manure piles?"

"I'm sure Grandpa will find plenty to keep you busy."

"He told me *you* were going to show me around."

Bobbie pushed her hat back. "I really hate to disappoint you, Al, but I'm leaving tomorrow. I'll be gone for more than a week chasing stray cattle in the brush country."

"The name is Alex."

"Like I said, *Alex,* every year, after we gather in the flats, we go up in the hills to look for wild cows."

"Oh gee," Alex mocked, "and I was really looking forward to getting to know you better —cousin."

Bobbie held the suitcase out in front of her and let it drop at Alex's feet. "Yeah, it's too bad there's not going to be time for that."

CHAPTER 2

The next morning Bobbie was up early. Grandpa was already downstairs making breakfast. She took the stairs two at a time and burst into the kitchen.

"It won't work, Grandpa. She's so green . . . you know how it is up there. She won't last a day."

"I told her she could go."

Bobbie could hear the final edge in her grandpa's voice. But she couldn't help trying one more time. "What if she can't ride?"

"She rides. She's been to one of those equestrian schools."

Bobbie knew it was useless. She sighed and headed for the barn. When her grandpa made a decision, that was it. She would just have to get used to the idea of baby-sitting her cousin for the next week. She threw a feed can across the barn and it crashed into the wall above the door.

Alex stepped inside the barn. This morning she was wearing a denim Western shirt over a red T-shirt, a pair of stiff new jeans, and new boots. "Watch your temper there, pard, you nearly hit me." She moved forward and half turned. "Gramps bought them for me," she said, gesturing at her clothes. "How do I look?"

The side of Bobbie's mouth went up but she didn't say anything.

"Gramps said I should come out and see if you need any help."

Bobbie chewed the inside of her lip. "If you're coming with me, you better get ready. I'm leaving in a half hour. I already fed your horse. He's the strawberry roan in the pen. Saddles are in the tack shed."

Bobbie moved past her cousin and grabbed a tarp off a peg on the wall. She took it outside and wrapped it in her bedroll.

In a few minutes Alex returned, leading the roan. Bobbie frowned. The horse's back was still bare. "I told you the saddles are in the tack shed—over there."

"All I could find were Western saddles. I'm used to riding English."

"You mean those itty-bitty things with hardly any leather on 'em and no saddle horn?"

Alex nodded.

"Look, Al, we're not going on an Easter egg hunt. We're looking for stray cattle. Some of them are mean and all of them are wild. You'll be spending whole days in the saddle. Maybe you should tell Grandpa you want to stay here until I get back. It'll only be a week."

"You wish." Alex turned and led the roan toward the tack shed again. "Don't worry about me, hotshot. If you can handle it, so can I."

Bobbie tightened the cinch on Sonny, the big sorrel gelding that was her favorite roping horse. "Looks like we're in for it, old boy." She fastened the saddlebags and headed for the house.

In the yard, she stopped to give Wolf a pat.

He really was part wolf. Bobbie had raised him from a pup and he adored her.

She walked into the house. The screen door slammed behind her. "That you, Bobbie?" Her grandpa came in from the kitchen. "You kids about ready?"

"She's a flake, Grandpa. And besides, she rides English."

"Give her a chance, Bobbie. Look, if they took you to Los Angeles and turned you loose, you wouldn't have a clue. How smart you are depends on what part of the world you happen to be standing on at the time."

The screen door opened. Alex poked her head in. "I'm ready, Wyatt."

"Wyatt?"

"You know. As in—you make me *urpp*." Alex winked at their grandfather.

Bobbie's face turned red. She thought about dragging Alex outside and settling their feud right then. But one look at Grandpa told her it wouldn't be a wise move. Instead she said, "I guess we're ready, then."

Grandpa followed them out to the horses. Bobbie whistled for Wolf, checked her cinch, and swung into the saddle. "See you in a week, Grandpa . . ."

She looked over at Alex, who was riding the roan in circles, bobbing up and down in the saddle, English style.

Bobbie sighed. ". . . if not before."

CHAPTER 3

The girls rode in silence up a sandy canyon bed for a couple of miles; then Bobbie turned onto a narrow trail to the right. Cattle had climbed the embankment for years and hollowed out a path up the steep canyon wall.

Wolf stayed close. Sometimes they couldn't see him, but he was always within easy calling range.

The path soon became more rugged. Bobbie ducked under a piñon limb that had grown over the trail. It hit Alex full in the face and dragged her off the back of the horse. She landed in the only mud puddle in the whole trail.

The frightened old roan jumped forward a few steps and then stopped, waiting patiently for Alex to get up.

Bobbie turned in the saddle. "Are you okay?"

Alex had a red welt across her cheek. She glared at her cousin. "You did that on purpose." Shaking, she slung some of the mud off her hands, wiped the rest on her pants, and grabbed the reins.

A cow was bawling somewhere down the canyon. Without a word Bobbie sank her spurs into Sonny and loped toward the cliff. The horse lunged off the ledge and landed back in the bottom of a sandy gully with Wolf right on his heels.

Bobbie quickly spotted the cow behind a salt cedar. She was a big cow with a two-month-old heifer calf. Bobbie shook out her rope into a good-sized loop, gave it a couple of twirls, aimed, and let go. The rope landed easily around the calf's neck. Bobbie dallied around the saddlehorn and backed Sonny up a few steps. Then she turned and started up the trail, leading the calf, with the cow following close behind. "Bring 'em up, Wolf."

Alex was back on the roan, waiting in the middle of the trail. When she saw the cow she smirked and said, "Find one of your long-lost relatives?"

"The only relative I have up here is a mud hen, and she's fixing to get run over if she's stupid enough to stay in the middle of the trail."

Bobbie didn't wait for Alex to get out of the way. She pushed past, dragging the calf. The roan pinned Alex's leg against the side of the embankment. The excited cow ran past and kicked backward. She nailed Alex square on the kneecap.

"It's not too late for you to turn back, Al." Bobbie smiled sweetly over her shoulder. "Just follow the canyon down and you'll be fine."

Alex gritted her teeth and tried not to show how much her knee hurt. "Listen, Bobbie, I'm in. Get it through your thick head, there's nothing you can do to get rid of me."

"Why is it so important for you to be up here? You obviously like me about as well as I like you, so what's the big attraction?"

"Maybe it's because I know how much it bothers you that I'm here."

Bobbie shrugged. "It's your funeral." She trotted ahead. The cow and calf had to run to keep up, which meant that Alex had to ride in a cloud of choking dust.

A mile and a half later, they topped out in a meadow completely surrounded by a thick wall of trees. Ancient run-down wooden corrals stood in the middle of the grassy pasture.

Bobbie rode her horse into one of the pens, closed the gate, and let the calf go. She stepped off and led Sonny to the water tank. It was bone-dry. She reached down and turned a valve. Clear spring water gushed into the tank.

"If I were you, Al, I'd water my horse. He's had a long trip." Bobbie let Sonny have a long cool drink.

Alex slid out of the saddle. She walked a bit stiffly and bowlegged as she led the roan to water. Bobbie couldn't help smiling.

"What are you laughing at?" Alex snapped.

"How long have you had it?"

"What?"

Bobbie pointed at her and laughed harder. "Arthritis of the rump."

"I've had enough." Alex let go of her horse and hit Bobbie like a tigress, driving her back and knocking her on her rear. "Now we'll see if *you* have problems with *your* rump."

Bobbie leapt to her feet. Her lips were tight. She stalked past Alex and as she did reached out and shoved her backward.

Into the water tank.

Alex stood up. Her clothes were sopping wet. She shook the water off, pushed her hair out of her eyes, and climbed out. Bobbie was doubled over, laughing.

Alex was steaming. She swung at Bobbie, clipping her on the jaw. Bobbie tried to grab her arm but missed. Alex punched her again, this time in the face. Blood spurted from Bobbie's nose.

The fight was on. Wolf ran back and forth barking furiously as the girls rolled on the ground, each one trying to get a better grip on the other, until they wound up underneath the roan. The horse snorted and danced nervously, trying to avoid them. Suddenly he jumped sideways and came down hard with his front hooves.

Right on Bobbie's ankle.

CHAPTER 4

The orange flame of the fire flickered against the dark night. Bobbie dug her spoon into a can of cold pork and beans. She put some on the grass for Wolf.

Alex studied Bobbie's wrapped ankle in silence. Then she lay back on her bedroll and closed her eyes. "My dad didn't tell me being a cowboy was so much *fun*."

"Your dad?" Bobbie put down the spoon. "I thought he was some kind of bank executive."

"He is, but he used to work this ranch when he was a kid—along with your dad. That's the real reason I'm here. He's always had this big guilt thing about not being around for Gramps when your dad died and he has this stupid idea that somehow I'll suddenly turn into Annie Oakley and make up for it."

"He doesn't need to worry. You're no Annie Oakley, and me and Grandpa do just fine without anybody's help."

"I said it was stupid. Besides, my dad looked into the ranch records. He thinks the Rocking W is about to go under."

Bobbie stared at the fire in silence, then sighed. "Sometimes it gets awful close. That's why I come up and get these strays every year. The money they bring always seems to keep us out of hot water. This year, though, I have to admit, things are a little closer than usual."

"What are you going to do now?"

"What I came up here for."

"How? That ankle is bruised so bad you can't even walk. You're lucky it's not broken. You wouldn't even be over here if I hadn't dragged you."

Bobbie's jaw thrust out. She sat up. "You didn't drag me, you only helped me. I could outwalk you any day of the week." She stopped, then smiled sheepishly, looking at her ankle. "Although you did a good job wrapping up my foot."

Alex shrugged. "You're welcome."

Bobbie used her pocket knife to open a can of peaches. "So, what's it like in Los Angeles?"

"It's great. There's always something going on."

"Like what?"

"Stuff. You know, hanging out."

"Hanging out? Of what, a window?"

Alex frowned. "Are you serious?"

Bobbie stuffed peaches in her mouth. "If you don't want to tell me, just forget it."

"Hanging out is . . . being with your friends. Sometimes we go to down to the mall and just sort of stand around."

Bobbie rubbed Wolf behind the ears. "And you think that's fun?"

"We do other stuff. Sometimes we get into a good game of asphalt football, no rules."

Bobbie stared at her.

Alex stared back. "What? You thought all I did was sit around and paint my nails?" She threw a stick into the fire. "What do you do with your friends, besides all this cowpoke junk?"

"The only kids who live around here are from the Bledsoe place. You passed it coming in."

"You mean that fancy ranch with the two-story house and the white pipe fences?"

"That's the one. They have two boys close to my age but they're both jerks. I keep to myself most of the time. In the summer, I usually break a colt or two, that keeps me busy. Sometimes on Saturday, Grandpa and I go see a movie."

"Sounds kinda tame."

Bobbie eased her ankle up on the swells of her saddle. "We'll see how tame you think it is this time tomorrow."

Chapter 5

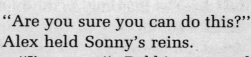

"Are you sure you can do this?" Alex held Sonny's reins.

"I'm sure." Bobbie stepped into the stirrup on the wrong side of her horse to avoid using her swollen ankle. "Get on your horse. If we see any cattle, I'll do the roping. You and Wolf get behind and push them."

Bobbie led the way out of the meadow through a thick stand of trees. "When we see one she'll probably run. We'll have to move fast or we'll lose her in the brush." She looked back at Alex over her shoulder. "By the way, you're gonna need to learn to duck."

Alex grabbed a pine cone from a nearby tree and threw it at the center of Bobbie's back.

Bobbie shook her rope out and held it close. A flash of black ran across the trail in front of them. "There goes one. Come on."

Sonny bolted after the cow. Trees went by in a blur. The cow was wild and had no intention of letting them come anywhere near her.

They raced over one ridge and started up the next. Alex did her best to keep up. Most of the time she just held on and let the roan decide where to go. The cow made a quick left and the roan nearly lost Alex. Her feet were out of the stirrups and she barely hung on.

Bobbie waited for a clearing. She would only have one chance, and when they exploded out into a small opening she threw her loop. It caught the cow's horns. Sonny stopped dead, and when the black cow hit the end of the rope, she flipped around facing them.

The cow was mad. She fought and pulled and tried to back up. Sonny held her fast. Then the cow made a wild dash around a tree. Bobbie let her fight with the tree until the animal was worn out. Then she calmly rode around the tree and led her captive back toward the meadow.

Wolf and Alex fell in behind. "Are we going to do this for every single one?" Alex asked, breathing heavily.

Bobbie nodded. "Unless you have a better idea."

"At this rate, we'll be up here a month."

"Grandpa and I did it different when he used to come up with me."

"Was it faster?"

"Yeah, but I don't think you'll like it."

"Anything would beat this."

"Cows generally will stick together if you get a few rounded up. If you think you can handle it, I'll go get them and bring them back here to you. Your job will be to keep them together until we have enough to move down to the corrals . . ." She trailed off, waiting for Alex's answer.

"How hard can it be?"

Bobbie smiled mischievously. She pulled Sonny to a stop, giving some slack in the rope. "Take the loop off this one and I'll go hunt you another one."

Alex stepped down and cautiously approached the cow. Alex jerked the rope up and off the horns. The instant the cow was free she took off like a shot.

"Don't just stand there." Bobbie re-coiled her rope. "Go get her. I'll be back with another one in a few minutes. Come with me, Wolf." She smacked Sonny on the rump with the rope and the horse loped off.

Alex scrambled to the roan and climbed on. She could still hear the black cow ahead of her—somewhere—crashing through the brush.

CHAPTER 6

Bobbie was dragging an obstinate bull calf down the trail to the spot where she had left Alex. The calf still hadn't learned that it was easier to follow than to dig in and make Sonny drag him. Wolf nipped the calf's hind leg and then ran back to make sure the mama cow was still following.

Bobbie really didn't know what she'd expected to see when she got back—but she knew this wasn't it.

Alex's red T-shirt was hanging in a tree. It had a big brown arrow on it drawn with mud, pointing west.

Bobbie pushed her hat up and scratched her forehead. "What? . . ."

She grabbed the T-shirt and headed in the direction the arrow indicated. The calf struggled but Sonny was so powerful it didn't matter.

From the top of the next ridge she saw them. Alex and the roan were guarding the entrance to a box canyon just below. Three mama cows with calves were munching on grass in front of her.

Bobbie laughed out loud. "Well, what do you know." She moved down in the canyon and rode up beside the roan.

Alex jumped down and took the rope off the bull calf. She tried to act casual. "We ran across these extras on our way here. I thought we might as well bring them along."

"Amazing." Bobbie shook her head. "I forgot about this box canyon. How'd you find it?"

"Actually, the cow found it. I thought I'd never catch up with her, so I went back and left you that sign." She took the T-shirt Bobbie held out to her. "When I finally found her she was with these others. When they saw me they ran in here and the roan and I trapped them." Alex patted the horse's neck. "We make a pretty good team."

Bobbie snorted and shook her head. "We've been lucky, dumb lucky. But maybe we ought to test our luck by going after Diablo next."

"Diablo?"

"He's a wild bull. And big. Over two thousand pounds. Every year I go after him but so far he's always managed to get away. One year he hooked my horse, nearly killed him." Bobbie showed her the scar on Sonny's shoulder. Then she looked her cousin in the eye. "If we could get him, he'd be worth a lot."

Alex shrugged. "I'm game."

"Okay. But if I manage to bring him in, it'll be your job to keep him."

CHAPTER 7

"Get out of the way!"

Alex could hear barking, and pounding hooves coming at her. She pushed the roan close to the canyon wall.

Bobbie and Wolf shot past her. Seconds behind them was the ugliest, meanest-looking animal Alex had ever seen in her life. The bull was enraged and obviously bent on destroying Bobbie.

Bobbie jerked Sonny up short behind a boulder. The bull stopped, snorted at Wolf, pawed the ground, and prepared to charge.

Alex put two fingers in her mouth and

blew. The whistle pierced the air. The bull raised his head and looked around. For the first time he noticed the cows standing off to the side. He looked back at Bobbie, bellowed, and blew snot on the ground. Then he turned and trotted over to inspect the herd.

"I thought *you* were supposed to bring *him* in. Alex led the roan to the boulder. "Looks like it worked the other way around."

"That was close." Bobbie wiped sweat off her forehead with her sleeve. "Thanks for distracting him."

Alex's eyes widened. "Do my ears deceive me, or did I just hear Bobbie Walker say thank you?"

Bobbie ignored her. "I surprised Diablo in the brush just up the trail. He didn't care for it much and started after us. Figured if he was going to chase me anyway, I'd lead him back here."

Alex looked over at the big bull, which was now standing quietly with the rest of the herd. "How do we convince him to go with us to the pens?"

"As long as he's with the cows, we won't

have much trouble from him. But don't crowd him. We'll edge around and start them out of the canyon. Then I'll move up to the side. You and Wolf stay behind and push them out. Just remember—take everything nice and slow."

Chapter 8

They had fourteen head in the pen, including Diablo. Bobbie was trying to put the enormous bull in a separate pen. Both girls were still on their horses, trying to cut the bull out and force him into the next corral. Wolf had been ordered to stay out of the way.

"Try to get around on the other side. Work them easy. Careful, don't get too close to him." Bobbie shouted instructions as she moved around Diablo.

The bull snorted and pawed the ground. He ran straight at Sonny. But the big sorrel had played this game before. He quickly side-stepped and let the bull go past into the other pen.

Before the bull realized what had happened, Alex jumped down and pushed the gate shut behind him. She wiped the sweat and dirt off her face and leaned tiredly against the gate.

"Man, am I glad this day's over."

Bobbie looked at the sky. "We still have some daylight. Better stay after it till dark."

"You're not thinking of going back up there and finding more cows tonight, are you?"

"No. We've got plenty to do right here. Those calves need branding, and we ought to go ahead and castrate that bull calf and de-horn that one over there." Bobbie pointed across the pen.

Alex wasn't listening. She had her back turned and was watching Diablo. The bull's eyes were blood-red and he was still snorting and running around in circles.

"My dad told me people used to actually ride those things."

"What? Bulls? They still do. Mostly in rodeos now, though." Bobbie glanced over at Alex. "I've tried it a couple of times."

"Get real."

"I have. At the Fourth of July Rodeo. It's really not so bad. Hittin' the ground is what hurts."

"Are you serious? You couldn't get me on something like that for a million bucks."

Bobbie nodded. "I understand. You have to have backbone to ride bulls."

Alex's eyes narrowed. "What do you mean by that?"

"Nothing. It's just that you gotta be tough to ride bulls, that's all."

Alex stared through the wooden rails at Diablo. "You did it?"

"Sure."

Alex climbed up on the gate. "You rope him. I'll get on him."

"Hey, I was talking about normal bulls. This one's loco. He'll kill you."

Wolf growled. The hair on his back was standing up. A deeper voice cut the evening air. "Yeah, Bobbie. And we wouldn't want the new little girl hurt, now would we?"

Bobbie turned. Two boys were sitting on horses looking down the side of the hill at them.

"Calvin and Jesse Bledsoe," Bobbie said, her voice flat. "What are you two doing on Rocking W land?"

Jesse, the older and meaner Bledsoe boy, sneered. "It's a free country, Walker." He rode his gray horse to the corral fence and peered over it at the cattle. "Some of our cows have turned up missing and we thought they might have wandered over here. We're just checking."

"If we run across anything of yours we'll send it back your way."

"I just bet you will." Calvin, the younger boy, who was about Bobbie's size, spit a wad of tobacco juice on the ground. The brown liquid dribbled down his chin. "After you stamp the Rocking W brand all over them."

Bobbie forgot about her swollen ankle. She flew over the fence and pulled Calvin off his horse. Before the boy had time to react, Bobbie was sitting on his stomach and had his arms pinned to the ground.

36

Jesse started to step off his horse.

"I wouldn't do that if I were you." Alex pointed to Wolf. The dog was snarling and baring his teeth.

Bobbie let Calvin up and dusted off her jeans.

Alex moved to the top rail of the fence. "I'm new at all this cowboy stuff, but if I see either one of you around here again, I'm gonna let Wolf have you for supper. Understand?"

Calvin picked up his hat and glared at Bobbie. "This ain't the end of it, Walker."

The two boys mounted, wheeled their horses, and rode off. When they were out of sight Bobbie turned to Alex.

"Let Wolf have them for supper?"

Alex shrugged. "I read it in a book. It worked, didn't it?"

Bobbie couldn't help smiling. "Yeah, I guess it did."

CHAPTER 9

"This is crazy. Besides, it's fixing to rain. We better get the tarp out and make a tent or we're going to get wet."

"In a minute." Alex was balancing on the top rail of Diablo's pen. Waiting.

"I don't know how I let you talk me into this. I'm going to get my rope off of him and get ready for the rain." Bobbie started to climb the fence.

"Get back. Here he comes."

The bull had been mad about being penned up. But he was even madder now that he had a rope around his neck and two humans were practically in the pen with him. He charged at the fence. Alex saw her chance and jumped, landing squarely on his back just to the rear of his shoulders.

For a split second the bull was so surprised he didn't move. Then suddenly his temper flared and he went wild. Alex barely caught the rope before Diablo started bucking.

There was nothing else to hang on to. Alex clenched her knees as tight as she could, closed her eyes, and held on.

The bull was infuriated. He pitched up and down, sideways and around. But Alex managed to stay with him.

Bobbie couldn't believe it. She waved her hat in the air. "Yee-haw. Hook 'em, snotty! Stay with him, Alex. You got the old booger beat."

Then it ended. In a beautiful arc Alex flew through the air.

Into the water tank—again.

The bull turned and started for her. Alex tore up the fence and fell over the other side.

She was breathing hard when Bobbie got to

her and pounded her on the back. "You're a natural, cousin. Best ride I've seen in a while. And that dismount was something else."

Alex took in air.

Bobbie waited until Alex was breathing normally again and walked her to the camp. "You were great. A lot of first-time riders throw their guts up. Really, one time I saw Toby Matlock throw up for a half hour. It was gross. He musta had spinach for lunch because it was all slimy and green. . . ."

Alex held her stomach, gulped, swallowed. "You're not helping things here."

Thunder rumbled and Bobbie looked up. The clouds were black. The rain would be here any second. She quickly moved the saddles under a tree and covered the bedrolls with the tarp.

A drop hit Alex on top of the head.

Bobbie motioned for her to get underneath the tarp. "We don't have time for a tent. We'll be dry enough under here."

"Speak for yourself. You're not the one who just went for a swim in the water tank."

When the rain came it was as if someone

had tipped over a huge bucket of water. The two cousins moved down in their bedrolls with Wolf snuggled in between. They held on to the edges of the tarp so that it wouldn't blow away.

"Bobbie?"

"What?"

"Next time I start to do something that stupid, I want you to—"

Lightning crashed and Bobbie couldn't hear the rest of Alex's request. She grinned to herself and went to sleep.

Chapter 10

The rain stopped about midnight and all the clouds were gone by morning. Except for the wet grass and mud, it was as if it had never happened.

Bobbie pushed the tarp back and peeked out. Wolf licked her face. The sky was bright and blue overhead. She stood up and stretched.

She stopped. Something wasn't right, some sound was missing. She turned to the corral.

The cows were gone.

She ran to the pens. The gate was down, trampled in the mud.

Alex came up behind her, still rubbing the sleep out of her eyes. "I guess the lightning spooked them."

Bobbie moved inside the first pen. "That's what they wanted us to think."

"They? What are you talking about?"

"The Bledsoes. They did this."

"How can you tell?"

"The cattle might have run through the gate all right, but Diablo didn't open his own pen and follow them. Look over there."

Alex turned to look where Bobbie pointed. Diablo's pen was empty and the gate was standing wide open. "Those morons. Hadn't we better go after them?"

"On what? They took our horses."

Alex looked at the grassy hill where Bobbie had staked the horses the night before. They were gone too. All that was left were the girls' saddles and bedrolls.

Alex rubbed her hands together as she thought. "You know this country better than I do. Where do you think they took them?"

"It doesn't matter. We can't go after them on foot."

"Why not? Your ankle seems better this morning. Besides, we don't have horses in L.A. and we manage to get around." She moved to the saddles, untied Bobbie's saddle-bags, which held the food, and slung them over her shoulder. "You in or out, cowgirl?"

Bobbie ran her hand through her hair. She let out a deep breath and then whistled for Wolf. "I thought you told me to stop you when you wanted to do something stupid."

"They're your cows, aren't they?"

Bobbie nodded.

"You said the ranch might go under if you don't get them, didn't you?"

Bobbie nodded again.

"Then what's stupid about it? We need to go get them."

Bobbie untied her rope from the front of her saddle. "How can anybody argue with logic like that?"

45

CHAPTER 11

"Are you sure you know where you're going?" Alex leaned on a nearby boulder.

Bobbie sat beside her. "Like I said, it's a shortcut."

"I hope it beats your last shortcut."

"Give me a break. How was I supposed to know that canyon would be full of running water? I didn't know it had rained that hard up here."

"How soon before we get to this 'Turkey Roost,' anyway?"

"Not long. Just over the next ridge."

"What makes you think that's where the cows are?"

"The Bledsoes wouldn't take them home because it would be too easy for them to get caught. They're not smart enough to think of using the box canyon. So that leaves the Turkey Roost. It's the only other place on this whole mountain with even a piece of a fence that will hold cattle."

Alex stood up. "If we're that close, let's get going."

Bobbie's shoulders drooped. Her ankle was starting to throb and she noticed that her breathing was a little ragged. "I can't remember the last time I walked this far."

"That's because you're spoiled. Every time you step out of the house you probably jump on a horse."

Bobbie thought about telling Alex a thing or two about being spoiled. Then she remembered the morning she had actually tried to do her chores while riding Sonny. She half smiled and decided to save it for another time.

"Listen." Alex held up her hand. "Do you hear that?"

Wolf's ears were up. He was alert and started for the next ridge.

Bobbie called him back. She tried to get a grip on her breathing. "It's the cattle. They're bawling because those idiots have them penned up with no water."

Alex stayed low and climbed to the top of the ridge. She could see the cows. They were in a small clearing just on the other side of some trees. Diablo wasn't with them. The Bledsoe boys had made camp and were sitting near the fire laughing about something.

Bobbie crawled up behind her. "I don't see the horses or the bull."

Alex worked her way around a stand of pine trees. She motioned for Bobbie to follow and pointed to a spot on the other side of the cattle. "The horses are over there. They're not even tied up." She spoke in a low voice. "They must not be too worried about us coming after them."

"They need to start worrying." Bobbie squared her shoulders and headed down the hill.

"Hold on." Alex grabbed the back of Bobbie's shirt. "We need a plan."

"Why? Aren't you the one who said they were my cows and I should just go get them?"

"If you go rushing down there, who knows what those two might do? They could turn the cattle loose and we'd wind up chasing them all over again."

The corner of Bobbie's mouth twitched furiously. "I know one thing, we're not going to get them back by standing around here talking about it all day."

"Right." Alex picked up the saddlebags and moved under a tree and sat down. She rummaged inside and pulled out a can of tomatoes. "Yechh. Don't you eat anything besides beans, peaches, and tomatoes?"

"You're going to eat at a time like this?"

Alex nodded. "Those guys aren't going anywhere. Besides, it will give us time to make our plan."

CHAPTER 12

"This idea of yours better work." Bobbie stroked Wolf as she put her arm through the coiled rope.

"At least in the dark we have the element of surprise on our side."

They stood on the hill above the Bledsoes' camp. The fire had gone down to a dull glow. Both boys seemed to be asleep in their bedrolls. Alex could hear them snoring all the way to the top of the ridge.

The cousins made their way silently down the hillside and found their horses' halters and lead ropes in a heap next to a tree stump where the Bledsoes had tossed them. Bobbie handed Alex the roan's halter and moved to untangle Sonny's.

Alex slipped the halter over the roan's ears. The old horse seemed glad to see her. Alex patted him and scratched his neck.

They untied the Bledsoes' horses and pushed them gently away into the brush, then slipped Jesse's and Calvin's saddles onto their own mounts. Working silently, in a short time they were ready for the cows.

Across the opening, in the pale moonlight, Alex could see the Bledsoe boys still sleeping. She saw something else too.

Their boots.

Quickly she dismounted and tiptoed to the bedrolls.

Bobbie tried to grab her as she went past but Alex was too fast.

One pair wasn't enough. Alex reached for the second pair.

A large hand clamped around her ankle.

She fell forward.

The older Bledsoe had her foot. She twisted and threw the boots at him, pounding him in the chest and face. Jesse loosened his grip and Alex scrambled to stand up. He tackled her. The air blew out of her lungs. She felt as if someone had dropped a house on her.

Calvin sat up, reached his hand down the back of his long underwear, and scratched. He squinted out into the darkness. "What's going on, Jesse?"

"Get over here and help me, stupid. She's getting away!"

Alex squirmed out from under Jesse and managed to get to her knees. Calvin kicked off his sleeping bag and reached for her arm. She swung wildly with the other one.

Calvin yelled and held his eye. "She hit me!"

Bobbie rode up with Wolf by her side. The big dog snarled menacingly. "What do you think, Alex? Is it suppertime for Wolf?"

The boys froze as the dog neared them. Alex looked up. Bobbie was sitting on Sonny, laughing. She struggled to her feet, threw her hair back, and glared at Bobbie. "It took you long enough."

Bobbie smiled. "Yeah, I thought I better

bust this up before one of these poor boys got hurt." She turned to the Bledsoes. "Seems we have a small case of cattle rustling going on here." She rubbed her chin. "If I remember right, that's still a hanging offense."

"Want me to get a rope?" Alex asked.

Jesse shook his head nervously. "We were just having a good time with you, Bobbie. You know that. Shoot—we ain't no rustlers."

"Maybe we'll just let the sheriff decide about that, Jesse. Although it looks like a pretty clear-cut case to me."

Calvin looked worried. "Our dad will kill us if you call the law. He's running for county commissioner next month."

Alex moved beside Bobbie. "Maybe you clowns should have thought about that before you stole our cows."

"Our cows?" Jesse looked confused. "Who are *you*, anyway?"

Bobbie laughed. "Boys, I'd like you to meet another Walker. And in case you haven't figured it out yet—messing with her was probably the biggest mistake of your lives."

CHAPTER 13

Bobbie crawled out of her bed-roll the next morning to see Alex already saddling the horses.

"Too bad we lost Diablo," Alex said.

Bobbie shrugged. "There's always next year."

"Maybe we should stay up here a few more days and look for him."

"Naw. We better get these cows on home. Grandpa will start to get worried if we stay up here too long. And besides, we probably need to let somebody know about them." Bobbie pointed to a big pine tree. On either side was a Bledsoe, still dressed in his long underwear and tied securely to the trunk.

Jesse strained against the ropes. "You can't leave us here, Walker. There are bears up here."

"Don't worry," Alex yelled, "one sniff of you and they'll run the other way." She leaned close to Bobbie. "What are you really going to do with those two?"

"I figured we'd start the cows down the trail a ways and then I'd come back and untie them later."

Alex looked over at the boys. "Sure you don't want to go ahead and hang them?"

"It's tempting, but I guess I'll pass."

Alex pulled the barbed-wire gate open and the cows started filtering out. She stepped up onto her horse and began working to keep them bunched.

Bobbie watched her as she cut left to keep one of the calves from turning back. "Say, Alex, I was just wondering . . ."

Alex trotted closer. "What was that? I didn't hear you."

"I said I was just wondering about something."

"What?"

Bobbie cleared her throat and her mouth started twitching. "I was just thinking that if you weren't doing anything next spring . . ."

Alex's face broke into a grin.

CHAPTER 14

Bobbie leaned down from the saddle and pulled the mailbox open. She took out a handful of letters and shut the box. One was postmarked Los Angeles. She ripped it open.

Dear Bobbie,

Just a line to let you know I made it home okay. I told my friends all about you and we're agreed. You should break one less colt this summer and come out for a visit. I told them it wasn't your fault that you were a just a hick from the country and made them promise not to be too rough on you.

Of course you realize it might not be as exciting as watching flies on manure or going to a movie on Saturday night, but we'll see what we can do.

Seriously, I would like to see an old cowpoke like you try to stand up in a pair of Rollerblades. So let me know.

Alex

P.S.

By the way, what does "hook 'em, snotty" mean anyway?

Bobbie folded the letter and stuffed it inside her shirt pocket. "Shoot, Sonny," she said, "everybody knows that's what you yell to a rider before he mounts a bull." She smiled, remembering the sight of Alex on Diablo's back. "So what do you think, Sonny? Want to go to California and hang out?"

The big horse shook a fly off his neck.

"I know what you mean." Bobbie moved him into a slow lope. "On the other hand, maybe you and I *should* go on out there. We'd show those city slickers a thing or two for sure."

GARY PAULSEN
ADVENTURE GUIDE

RIDING

A horse is a large, strong, and beautiful animal. But remember, a horse not a plaything, and it can hurt you. Always stay by the front half of a horse's body, even when grooming or mounting. Never make any sudden movements. Horses scare easily.

Equipment is very important to riding. Your saddle should not only fit you comfortably, it should also fit your horse, leaving it free from *gall,* or rub marks. A bit should suit your skill and your horse's mouth. Reins should be made of a material you feel comfortable handling.

Mount your horse from the left side, remembering to stay well away from those back hooves. Place your left foot in the stirrup, hold the reins in your left hand, grab the saddle horn, and step up. Throw your right leg over the saddle.

Gather your reins in one hand. Leave enough slack so that you are not bearing down hard on the horse's mouth. To go forward, gently nudge the horse with the heels of your boots. To back up, pull the reins evenly straight back toward the saddle horn. To turn right or left, simply pull the reins in the direction you want to go. Make sure you are sitting up straight. Your heels should be down.

If you are an inexperienced rider, practice riding your horse at a walk in an enclosed area. Later you can move up to a faster gait. When you are finished with your ride, be sure to give the horse a good rubdown.

ROPING

Roping is a challenging test of technique and accuracy. There are more than a hundred different brands and styles of ropes. Beginners should choose an inexpensive nylon rope. Shake the rope out in the store and see how the loop hangs. If it's lopsided, don't buy it.

Start by practicing roping on the ground. If you're lucky enough to have a plastic steer or calf head that you can stick in a bale of hay to use as a target, great. If not, you may have to choose something different. Fence posts or bicycle handlebars work just fine. (Little brothers and sisters do not!)

Coil your rope from the straight end. If you are right-handed, hold the end with the loop in that hand, with your index finger pointed. Let the coils rest loosely in your left hand. (If you are left-handed, do the opposite.) Shake your loop out a little larger than your coils.

Twirl your loop over your head in a flat, circular motion. Point your index finger at the target and throw the loop as if you were throwing a rock. The coils should slide through your left hand. When the loop settles around the target, pull out the slack.

One important reminder: Horses can be dangerous. Do not attempt to rope from horseback unless both you and the horse are experienced.

Don't miss all the exciting action!

Read the other action-packed books
in Gary Paulsen's
WORLD OF ADVENTURE!

The Legend of Red Horse Cavern

William Little Bear Tucker and his friend Sarah Thompson have heard the eerie Apache legend many times. Will's grandfather especially loves to tell them about Red Horse—an Indian brave who betrayed his people, was beheaded, and now haunts the Sacramento Mountain range, searching for his head. To Will and Sarah it's just a story —until they decide to explore a newfound mountain cave, a cave filled with dangerous treasures.

Deep underground Will and Sarah uncover an old chest stuffed with a million dollars. But now armed bandits are after them. When they find a gold Apache statue hidden in a skull, it seems Red Horse is hunting them, too. Then they lose their way, and each step they take in the damp dark cavern could be their last.

Rodomonte's Revenge

Friends Brett Wilder and Tom Houston are video game whizzes. So when a new virtual reality arcade called Rodomonte's Revenge opens near their home, they make sure they're its first customers. The game is awesome. There are flaming fire rivers to jump, beastly buzz-bugs to fight and ugly tunnel spiders to escape. If they're good enough they'll face Rodomonte, an evil giant waiting to do battle within his hidden castle.

But soon after they play the game, strange things start happening to Brett and Tom. The computer is taking over their minds. Now everything that happens in the game is happening in real life. A buzz-bug could gnaw off their ears. Rodomonte could smash them to bits. Brett and Tom have no choice but to play Rodomonte's Revenge again. This time they'll be playing for their lives.

Escape from Fire Mountain

"*. . . please anybody . . . fire . . . need help.*"

That's the urgent cry thirteen-year-old Nikki Roberts hears over the CB radio the weekend she's left alone in her family's hunting lodge. The message also says that the sender is trapped near a bend in the river. Nikki knows it's dangerous, but she has to try to help. She paddles her canoe downriver, coming closer to the thick black smoke of the forest fire with each stroke. When she reaches the bend, Nikki climbs onshore. There, covered with soot and huddled on a rock ledge, sit two small children.

Nikki struggles to get the children to safety. Flames roar around them. Trees splinter to the ground. But as Nikki tries to escape the fire, she doesn't know that two poachers are also hot on her trail. They fear that she and the children have seen too much of their illegal operation—and they'll do anything to keep the kids from making it back to the lodge alive.

The Rock Jockeys

Devil's Wall.

Rick Williams and his friends J.D. and Spud—the Rock Jockeys—are attempting to become the first and youngest climbers to ascend the north face of their area's most treacherous mountain. They're also out to discover if a B-17 bomber rumored to have crashed into the mountain years ago is really there.

As the Rock Jockeys explore Devil's Wall, they stumble upon the plane's battered shell. Inside, they find items that seem to have belonged to the crew, including a diary written by the navigator. Spud later falls into a deep hole and finds something even more frightening: a human skull and bones. To find out where they might have come from, the boys read the navigator's story in the diary. It reveals a gruesome secret that heightens the dangers the mountain might hold for the Rock Jockeys.

Look for these thrill-packed adventures coming soon!

Danger on Midnight River

Daniel Martin doesn't want to go to Camp Eagle Nest. He wants to spend the summer as he always does: with his uncle Smitty in the Rocky Mountains. Daniel is a slow learner, but most kids call him retarded. Daniel knows that at camp things are only going to get worse. His nightmare comes true when he and three bullies must ride the camp van together.

On the trip to camp Daniel is the butt of the bullies' jokes. He ignores them and concentrates on the roads outside. He thinks they may be lost. As the van crosses a wooden bridge, the planks suddenly give way. The van plunges into the raging river below. Daniel struggles to shore, but the driver and the other boys are nowhere to be found. It's freezing, and night is setting in. Daniel faces a difficult decision. He could save himself . . . or risk everything to try to rescue the others too.

The Gorgon Slayer

Eleven-year-old Warren Trumbull has a strange job. He works for Prince Charming's Damsel in Distress Rescue Agency, saving people from hideous monsters, evil warlocks, and wicked witches. Then one day Warren gets the most dangerous assignment of all: He must exterminate a Gorgon.

Gorgons are horrible creatures. They have green scales, clawed fingers, and snakes for hair. They also have the power to turn people to stone. Warren doesn't want to be a stone statue for the rest of his life. He'll need all his courage and skill—and his secret plan—to become a true Gorgon slayer.

The Gorgon howls as Warren enters the dark basement to do battle. Warren lowers his eyes, raises his sword and shield, and leaps into action. But will his plan work?

Captive!

Roman Sanchez is trying hard to deal with the death of his father—a SWAT team member gunned down in the line of duty. But Roman's nightmare is just beginning.

One day during school masked gunmen storm into his classroom. Roman and three other boys are taken hostage. There's Jeff, captain of the football team; Mitch, president of the student council; and Woody "the Worm," class brainiac. Each boy has his own ideas about how to escape, but when they can't agree, their first chance is lost.

The boys are thrown into the back of a truck and hauled to a run-down mountain cabin miles from anywhere. They are bound with rope and given no food. Worst of all, it seems that the ransom the kidnappers have demanded is not going to be paid—making their deadly threats even more real.

Roman knows time is running out. Now he must somehow put his father's death behind him so that he and the others can launch a last desperate fight for freedom.

Project: A Perfect World

When Jim Stanton's family moves to a small town in New Mexico, everyone but Jim is happy. His father has a great new job as a research scientist at Folsum Laboratories. His mother has a beautiful new house. Folsum Labs even buys a bunch of brand-new toys for his little sister.

But there's something strange about the town. The people all dress and act alike. Everyone's *too* polite. And they're all eerily obedient to the bosses at Folsum Labs.

Though he has been warned not to leave town, Jim wanders into the nearby mountains looking for excitement. There he meets Maria, a mountain girl with a shocking secret that involves Folsum Laboratories, a dangerous mind-control experiment, and—most frightening of all—Jim's family.

CHART YOUR COURSE TO EXCITEMENT!

Take the journey of a lifetime with *Gary Paulsen World of Adventure!* Every story is a thrilling, action-packed odyssey, containing an adventure guide with important survival tips no camper or adventurer should be without!

Order any or all of these exciting **Gary Paulsen** adventures. Just check off the titles you want, then fill out and mail the order form below.